ALEXANDER
GETS A NEW
HOVERBOARD

Icey Shaikh

Every day after school, Alexander would meet up with his two best friends Robert and Hakeem. Robert lived in the house just next door to Alexander. Hakeem lived just across the street. They would all gather at Robert's house to decide how they wanted to play.

On this day, Robert said, let's all go to the park and ride our hoverboards. "Yes, said Hakeem,"! "I'll go get mine." Alexander shrugged his shoulders as he sadly proclaimed, "I don't have a hoverboard." Robert said, "you don't have a hoverboard"? Hakeem said, "well, do you know how to ride one"? Alexander shrugged his shoulders again.

Robert said, "no worries, Alexander." "Come along; we'll show you. So, the three friends headed to the neighborhood park, which was only down the block.

Robert and Hakeem took turns showing Alexander how to ride. Next, it was Alexander's turn. He was a little bit nervous in the beginning, but in no time at all, Alexander was spinning and turning. He rode up to the ramp then down the ramp. He even learned to ride on one foot. Alexander was a pro.

The three boys continued playing until almost sundown. Then they hurried back home because they all knew the rules, that they must be back indoors before dark.

At dinner, Alexander couldn't stop talking about the fun he had at the park today, riding the hoverboard.

While helping mom clear the table, Alexander popped the question. "Mom, will you buy me a hoverboard"? Mom said, "yes, I will buy it, but you'll have to earn money for it on your own." "I'm sure there are some odd jobs you can do around this house or for your neighbors to earn this money." "You can even ask your dad."

"Where should I start, said Alexander"? "You can sweep the floor and take out the trash said, mom." This act of obedience earned Alexander $3.00.

For the rest of the week, Alexander was busy raking neighbors' yards or taking out their trash. He even walked old man Fowler's puppy for $2.00. All the money he made; Alexander hid in a shoebox underneath his bed. He didn't have time to play with Robert and Hakeem now. He had to get his hoverboard.

Then dad came up with an idea. He told Alexander to buy a big box of assorted chips and drinks with the money he earned so far. Alexander could then come to work with dad and sell these chips and drinks to travelers in the hotel lobby.

So that evening, dad took Alexander to a nearby grocery store to buy the items.

The next morning after breakfast, mom packed a lunch for dad and Alexander, who then headed out to the hotel. Alexander had visited dad's hotel before but never with so much excitement.

Once they reached the hotel, dad helped Alexander set up a small booth in the corner of the hotel lobby with a banner that read "chips and ice-cold drinks for sale"!

At the end of the day, dad helped Alexander count all his money. $125. Dad was so proud of Alexander; he took him right away to the toy store.

Alexander hurried to the toy section, where he found his hoverboard in his favorite color blue. "Dad, dad, it's over here, yelled Alexander." "Calm down, son," said dad walking over to Alexander. "How much is it," asked dad? $135. Then Alexander looked worried. Dad said, "no problem, son, I'll pay the difference."

As dad picked up the hoverboard, Alexander cautioned, "be careful, don't bump it, don't drop it, handle it easy now"! Dad just grinned, but Alexander knew how hard he had worked and the weeks it took him to save.

The very next day, Alexander, Robert, and
Hakeem rode their hoverboards.

The End

Alexander Gets A New Hoverboard

iUniverse books may be ordered through booksellers or by contacting:

iUniverse
1663 Liberty Drive
Bloomington, IN 47403
www.iuniverse.com
844-349-9409

Because of the dynamic nature of the Internet, any web addresses or links contained in this book may have changed since publication and may no longer be valid. The views expressed in this work are solely those of the author and do not necessarily reflect the views of the publisher, and the publisher hereby disclaims any responsibility for them.

Any people depicted in stock imagery provided by Getty Images are models, and such images are being used for illustrative purposes only. Certain stock imagery © Getty Images.

ISBN: 978-1-6632-2004-2 (sc)
ISBN: 978-1-6632-2005-9 (hc)
ISBN: 978-1-6632-2006-6 (e)

Library of Congress Control Number: 2021905923

Print information available on the last page.

iUniverse rev. date: 03/19/2021

CPSIA information can be obtained
at www.ICGtesting.com
Printed in the USA
BVHW021403280122
627226BV00004B/40